In fact I think helping is
one of the things I am best at.

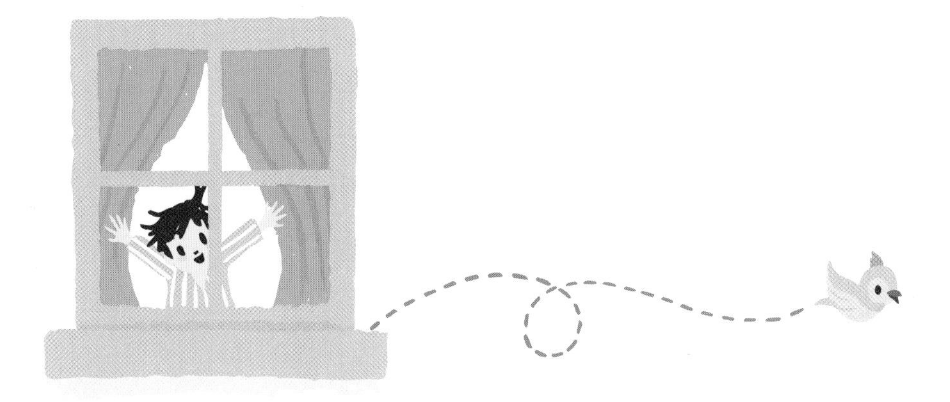

I start the day by helping everyone
wake up and get out of bed.

Mummy and Daddy find this rather tricky
so sometimes I have to help them
a little bit LOUDER.

When everyone is finally
up and zooming about
I like to help by getting
myself dressed.

And then I make breakfast.

Deeeeeeelicious!

After all that it's shoes on . . .

and off we pop!

At the shops I help Daddy find
everything we need.

And at the park I like to make sure that everyone is having as much fun as possible.

When we get home I even help
put the shopping away.

After all that helping I can get a bit exhausted.
So I go and help the dog have a rest.

But soon enough I'm full of beans and helping out **all over** the place.

Organising Mummy's office . . .

and tidying up
with Daddy.

My brother is much, much littler than me,
so he needs lots of help . . .

with sharing . . .

dressing up . . .

and knowing
what's what.

When they come to visit I love to help Grandma with her make-ups and Grandpa with his hairstyles.

I mainly do this when they are asleep . . .

and they are mainly asleep so it
all works out terrrrrific!

I am always on the lookout for new
ways to be helpful. Like, maybe,
jazzing up the dog . . .

or making Daddy's shoes
a bit more snazzy.

. . . or even brightening the place up a bit!

Sometimes I have to remember
NOT to be quite so helpful.

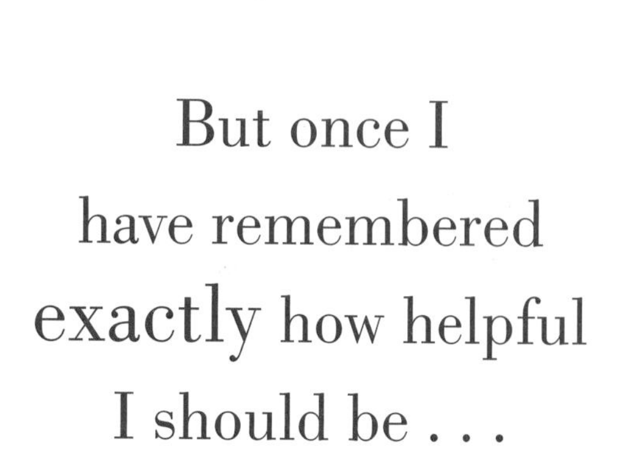

But once I
have remembered
exactly how helpful
I should be . . .

I can get back to being my best and helping everyone out again.

After all . . .

. . . I don't know what they'd do without me!

for Sarah Underhill

who really has been ever so helpful

PUFFIN BOOKS
UK | USA | Canada | Ireland | Australia | India | New Zealand | South Africa
Puffin Books is part of the Penguin Random House group of companies
whose addresses can be found at global.penguinrandomhouse.com.
www.penguin.co.uk www.puffin.co.uk www.ladybird.co.uk

First published 2017
001

Printed in China
A CIP catalogue record for this book is available from the British Library
Hardback ISBN: 978–0–141–36500–8
Paperback ISBN: 978–0–141–36501–5
All correspondence to: Puffin Books, Penguin Random House Children's
80 Strand, London WC2R 0RL